AF669636

ACKNOWLEDGEMENT

Heartfelt gratitude to each of the talented co-authors who poured their hearts and souls into this anthology. Your collective creativity, passion and dedication have made **'Old Yet Golden'** a truly special collection of poems. Every word, every line, and every stanza is a testament to your inspired voices.

Special thanks to the **Artiverse** team for their invaluable guidance, unwavering support, and for providing us with this wonderful opportunity to showcase our work. Your expertise and encouragement have been instrumental in bringing this anthology to life.

We are grateful for the chance to share our words with the world, and we hope that 'Old Yet Golden' will touch hearts, spark emotions, and leave a lasting impression on all who read it.

With gratitude,
Tharthing Zimik
Compiler of Old yet Golden

DISCLAIMER

The compiler has made every effort to edit and refine the content. Despite our best attempts, some errors may still exist. We have taken measures to ensure originality, and plagiarism detection has been employed. The compiler, publication house, and associated parties disclaim any responsibility for the content. The authors are solely responsible for the accuracy and originality of their work.

ABOUT THE BOOK

Old Yet Golden is a poignant poetry anthology that explores timeless themes of friendship, heartbreak, love, and memories. Featuring 30 talented co-authors, this collection **is** a masterful blend of emotions, nostalgia, and reflections. Each poem is a beautifully crafted piece that echoes the past while resonating with the present. With its universal themes and diverse perspectives,
'Old Yet Golden' is a must-read for poetry lovers. Dive into this treasure trove of verse and let the emotions wash over you. A. treasure trove of feelings,
'Old Yet Golden' will touch your heart and linger in your mind."

OLD YET GOLDEN

The title 'Old Yet Golden' is inspired by my childhood home, where laughter echoed, memories were forged, and dreams took shape. Though its physical walls may no longer stand tall, the warmth, love and joy it shelte- red remain etched in my heart, forever treasured. I've since moved to a new home, one that's bigger, brighter, and more comfortable, but none can rival the happiness and nostalgia that old house evoked. I also dedicate this collection to all readers who shine bright like gold, bringing joy, value and light to the lives of those around them – may you continue to sparkle and inspire.

Warmly,
Tharthing Zimik
Compiler of Old yet Golden

About the Compiler

As a kid, she wished she was an author, but she never believed she would become one, largely due to the limited opportunities she had because of her physical disability. Born with a condition that left her 90% disabl- ed, **as** recognized by the government, she faced signifi- cant challenges **in** accessing education. Despite attend- ing school for only a year and a half in her entire life, her love for books and writing remained strong**. S**he proudly considered herself "**differently abled**" rather than "disabled." Inspired by **J.K**. Rowling's journey with the Harry Potter series – from being rejected to becoming a best-selling author – **s**he found the courage to pursue her passion. Rowling's story motivated her to turn her dreams into reality.

Today, she's featured in over 100+ anthologies and published her debut solo book, "**Pen Never Lies**." She now firmly believes that writing comes not just from academics**, b**ut mostly from the heart.

COMPILER'S WRITE-UP

The Last Petal of Cosmos

In sun-kissed gardens, where daylight softly plays,
Cosmos once unfurled, a petal-printed shawl.
The sky, enamored, blushed with pink, a lover's sigh
Their beauty – an incantation, whispered, yet words
deny.

Aerial kingdoms stirred, bees and butterflies did play,
Dancing on zephyrs, in rapturous, sun-kissed exuberant.
But ephemeral as morning dew, their splendor did wane,
Petal by petal, fading, till only one, forlorn, lingered on.

Now, in the vast, echoing garden, solitude does reign,
A single, trembling petal, clinging to its stem in
desperate strain.
The air, bereft of wings, no longer whispers secrets
sweet,
Silence, like a shroud, enfolds the space where beauty
used to dwell.

But still, She blooms with a cosmos' gentle smile,
Her spirit unbroken, like a verdant root that stays deep within.
Though petals fall, Her radiance remains, a steadfast presence,
Unfazed by life's tempests, She shines with joyous might.
Her eyes smiled softly on the Last Petal's gentle face.

Yet, in the secret pages of Her heart's diary,
A different tale is told, one of sorrow's heavy sigh.
From first to last, the lines are filled with pain,
No whisper of joy, no echo of happiness' sweet refrain.

~Tharthing Zimik

1. The Soul of Friendship

Friendship means sharing with heart so wide,
Standing together, side by side.
Helping in sorrow, laughing in light,
Holding each other through every fight.

I found a friend, so close, so true,
In joy and pain, we stuck like glue.
I trusted deep, I gave my all,
She held me up whenever I'd fall.

We cared, we laughed, we helped a lot,
Each memory now, a treasured thought.
But life turned strange, I don't know how,
Maybe fate had raised its brow.

One day someone stepped between,
With words so sharp, so cold, unseen.
She believed those lies, turned away,
Our bond just shattered that very day.

No more messages, no more calls,
Our friendship broke like crumbling walls.

She chose her path, I walk my own,
Yet still inside, I feel alone.

But friendship means much more than trust —
It’s loyalty, even when winds gust.
Not every whisper should shake your ground,
True friends don’t leave when doubt is found.

So here's to friendship, pure and bright —
May we be candles in each other’s night.
And even if some ties must end,
The lesson stays — be a true friend.

Lalita H
Email: lalitahebbar@gmail.com

2. **Jahanvi Singh**

Certainly! Here's the revised paragraph with "clinical psychologist" Jahanvi Singh hails from Bhopal and is currently pursuing a Bachelor's degree in Psychology (Honours) in her hometown. She is a passi- onate and ambitious individual, deeply dedicated to her goal of becoming a child psychologist. Alongside her academic pursuits, Jahanvi is a multitalented artist with a love for poetry writing, dancing, singing, mehendi design, and sketching. She is also a district-level swimmer. Her creative works have been featured in several anthologies, and she has earned numerous awards for her poetry and performances in open mic singing events.

Email: jahanvisinghapril11@gmail.com
Insta :guddan0411

<u>*True Friend or Just Show?*</u>

A true friend isn't one, you know,
Who just puts on a friendly show.
A true friend isn't one who won't
Listen to you, though you don't.

A true friend isn't one who tries
To fake the care, to tell sweet lies.
A true friend isn't one who'll praise
You blindly, just to earn some grace.

A true friend isn't one who takes
You for granted with no breaks.
A true friend isn't one who'd fail
To think for you beyond the veil.

A true friend isn't one who hides
The path that's right, the truthful guide.
A true friend isn't one who cheers
Your wrongs and fuels your hidden fears.

A true friend isn't one who goes
And leaves you without a goodbye, no.
A true friend isn't one who'd flee
When you need their company.

A true friend isn't one whose eyes
Lack the warmth where true love lies.
A true friend isn't one who'd stare
And miss the pain you're hiding there.

Who doesn't know what you might need,
Your silent cries, your inner plead.
A true friend doesn't fake or lie
With promises that fade and die.

So is that friend you have, true?
I wonder… Do they value you?
As for me, I truly boast,
Yes, I do have a true friend, close.

Do you? Think about it…

– Jahanvi Singh

3. **Dr. Richa Biswal**

Old Yet Golden | Artiverse

Dr. Richa Biswal is an Assistant Professor in the P.G. Department of English at Maharaja Purna Chandra Autonomous College, Mayurbhanj, Odisha. Her areas of interest include Indian poetics, comparative literature, and aesthetics. She has published several research articles and book chapters in reputed volumes. Passionate about teaching and research, she actively engages in interdisciplinary academic pursuits.

Email: richabiswal123@gmail.com

The House Where Friendship Lived

There stands a house on a weathered lane,
Where sunlit echoes still remain.
Its walls have heard the fiercest laughs,
And tears that broke in second halves.

The swing still creaks, the paint still peels,
Yet every crack, a truth reveals—
Of shared umbrellas in pouring skies,
Of truth exchanged without disguise.

We carved our names in bark and wall,
Not knowing years would change it all.
Your voice, once close like whispered light,
Now only visit late at night.

I hold your letters like old songs,
Their faded ink still sings strong.
You taught me love, you showed me grace,
You left—yet left a sacred place.

Time moved ahead, as time will do,
But nothing quite replaces you.
The world went on with ruthless pace,
Yet paused for me in your embrace.

So here I sit, the fire dim,
My eyes blur out the light and limb.
But when I speak of golden days,

Your name still burns, a soft, bright blaze.

Some friendships time may tear apart,
But yours remains etched in my heart.

~Dr. Richa Biswal

Letters to a Love That Left.

You left when rain was halfway done,

And left me chasing phantom sun.
Your coat still hangs behind the door,
As if you'll walk in like before.

Your laughter haunts the evening air,
I smell your scent, you're everywhere.
The tea turns cold, the bedsheet bare,
I talk to ghosts that aren't quite there.

I kept the ring you never gave,
Buried in dreams I couldn't save.
Yet in my sleep, your voice arrives,
Still soft, still sure, still so alive.

We danced once slow beneath the moon,
Too young to know it ends too soon.
Your promises were made of thread,
Too fine to hold the tears we shed.

Yet still I wear your name like gold,
Though time has made my hands grow old.
Love isn't gone, it only fades—
Into the light, into the shades.

Now every ache I feel is proof—
Of golden youth beneath this roof.

Old Yet Golden* | *Artiverse

Though you are gone and seasons change,
The heart remembers every range.

For heartbreak, too, in twilight's hold,
Can shimmer soft—still old, yet gold.

~Dr. Richa Biswal

4. **Saloni Khanna**

She is Saloni Khanna, hailing from Kolkata, she colors the canvas with her hues. She started writing since October. 2019 in Your Quote App. She has a positive outlook towards life. She has a solo book An Ode To Living and has various anthologies accredited to her name . She enlightens everyone with her wisdom. Her thoughts are painted on many prestigious platforms.

Connection

Old Yet Golden | Artiverse

The language of love
Has no definition
It's a pure connection
With two loving hearts.
The language of love
Is so pure
It cures all diseases.
The language of love
Can be spiritual
When we have direct connection with God.
The language of love
Is magical.
Love is only language every heart speaks.
Love can't be bought
It's priceless and free.
Love is the language
With full care
A simple smile touches one's soul.
Love breathes within our skin
It clears the pores of the skin
Beautifies our soul within.
The language of love, a treasure true
A gift that's given, a love that's new
It heals all wounds, it soothes all pain
A love that's pure, a love that's gained.
Through laughter, tears, and pain
Our connection remains unbreakable
For in each other, we find
A love that's unshakeable.
We may be miles apart

But our connection knows no bounds.
It's the warmth of a smile
That reaches across every mile
A hand to hold in times of need
A shoulder to lean on when we bleed.
We are connected with sacred thread
Our love is so profound.
A child is connected to her mother's umbilical cord
The lullabies so strong every word gets rebound
A new life found.

©Saloni Khanna

5. **R Madhumitha**

R.Madhumitha is a bilingual poet and short story writer from Tamilnadu. **She** loves to write poems in **E**nglish language. She is an MA English graduate and short story writer. Currently she is pursuing MBA (HR). Her books are as follows "My Wings of Poetry","My Shades of life", " en oor ", Karadi Kadhaigal", Love and loves another part unexplained ","Selva"," Mariyathai Raman stories ".

Email: madhumithavinetha3@gmail.com
Insta :Madhumitha Vinetha

<u>*Rowdy Lady*</u>

I know the fools
Who they rules
Their schools
The pools of tears
By the rhythms
Of some pears
No uplifting dogmas
Jumping they are
Trumpet they blow
Made me to look
To show
A girn
To win
the position they hold

~R.Madhumitha

<u>*Changed Events*</u>

I love to go outside for rice and some sort of small small snacks and some sort of chips, I like flowers especially roses.
I like my head covered with roses.

Before some years a temple elephant
will come for getting money and fruits.

In our old rented house during rainy seasons so sewage water will enter the balcony.Those days even if I think there were more struggles.

~R.Madhumitha

6. Pavithra

She is Pavithra, a writer and a co author in this anthology. She thank the publication for giving her a chance to participate in this anthology.

Email: sparkepurlpublication@gmail.com
Insta: ourhome_sparke_purl

Love

I loved you in a way,
I want to be loved.
You loved me in a way,
You shall pass your time,
Just so freely.

Friendship

Ofcourse friend don't wanna stay together forever,
but if he shall leave any time,
why he is making friends?,
he shall choose to be alone,
without worrying others.

7. Fatema Ghodi

She is a girl who recently completed her schooling. She loves to pen down her thoughts.creativity is her hobby. Badminton is her favorite sport. She loves to explore new things. It's her first write up.

Email: fatemaghodi65@gmail.com

Slowly the time passes by;
we grow older.
No matter what the time is;
We stand shoulder to shoulder for each other
Deepest laughs and silent smiles;
The sorrows that fade away by togetherness.
No matter how much people come and go;
but the old one is yet golden..
In the dictionary of friendship;
The word separation never exists.
No matter where the life takes;
Old ones remain unforgettable.
From childhood to adulthood;
in whole journey, our bond was real.

~Fatema Ghodi

8. **Chetan Sarvagod**

He is a very good poet

Email: chetansarvagod7@email.com

A Special Friend

My one special friend - a feeling that is beyond words
There is a special person in my life who has given me everything - his time, his company, and most annoyingly, his true heart. He is an example of a form of friendship that is rarely seen in today's times.
I thought I had a volatile nature.
Sometimes my anger goes beyond limits,
but that friend of mine never paid attention to my anger, rather kept me in friendship with his love, understanding and patience. I have felt the need to recognize myself many times in life - sometimes financially, sometimes scientifically - but every time the one who was there stood by me without saying anything. From medicine to every heartache, he understood my every addiction and supported me without any literature.She knew me only as a friend, not as a name - she loved me as a mother, as a companion, as a brother, as a companion and even as her innocent son. It is no less than a miracle that so many different things were found in one person.
There were many days when my brokenness created a wall between us. The conversation stopped, the mechanic went home...
But every time, it was him w

ho took the first step, forgave me, hugged me and said -
"You are fine the way you are. Just don't leave me."
She is a part of my life, I can never imagine her absence.
I love her immensely. I stand by her in every way, no matter how rough the doors are.

If she needs anything - help, support, or just a smile - I am always with her in my heart.
She loves me a lot too. Sometimes she laughs at my naivety, sometimes she makes me understand, and sometimes she just holds my hand, as if to say -
"You are not alone, I am always there."
She has taught me the true meaning of life -
To love, forgive, tolerate and play.
I am grateful for her every day.
Not everyone gets a friend like her.
She is not just my friend, but my soul's friend.

Thank you for coming into my life.
Your friendship is my biggest strength.

~Chetan Sarvagod

8. ***Asra***

Asra writes to remember, and sometimes to forget. She writes what refuses to stay buried in her head. Her words carry fragments of silence, gathering moments that slip too easily through the hands. **She** believes every poem is a conversation with someone she may never meet, and every line is a small attempt at keeping something alive.

Email: asratufail1208@gmail.com
Insta: ethereal.lumos

<u>Grains That Remember</u>

I walked barefoot
on the sand
spilled from hourglass.

it burned,
as if each grain
had swallowed
a piece of the sun.

Should I blame the sun,
the sand,
or the hourglass
that shattered quietly,
letting time spill
in a slow golden flood?

The grains whispered
in the language of heat,
carrying the ghost
of our fingerprints.
They remembered us
better than we remembered ourselves.

When your absence
raised flickers
it cooled them,
emptied your voice,
left us tasting
like bitter truths.

Then, suddenly,
they felt wet.
Perhaps the sand
wept with us,
or perhaps

it simply mistook
our pain as rain.

Once,
we were the same beetles,
small and certain,
digging the same tunnels
through the same dust,
dreaming of flight.

When we finally grew wings,
And became butterflies
we noticed
that the wind was different
for each of us.
You flew east,
And I went west.
two different butterflies,
forgetting the soil
that once held
our restless shells.
We left.

~Asra

10. Dorcas Chigodho

Dorcas is a passionate poet with a gift for weaving words into emotional tapestries. With a keen eye for detail and a deep understanding of the human experience, Dorcas' poetry explores themes of love, memory, and the complexities of life. Through her writing, she invites readers to reflect on their own journeys and find solace in the shared human experi- ence.

Email: chigododorcas96@gmail.com

MEMORIES

Moments linger, fleeting and brief,
In this whirlwind of life's design,
Mesmerizing, yet ephemeral as a leaf.
Let joy fill the voids, and love entwine;
It's worth the time we share, the memories we weave.

It's hard to let go, as time's relentless pace
Steals moments from our grasp, leaving only space
For reminiscing the memoirs we hold dear,
The sweet symphonies of laughter, loud and clear,
The whispers of our hearts, the tears that fell like rain,
And the tantrums that awakened love's refrain.

This is not by chance, but living life's refrain,
Embracing every moment, joy and pain,
As our bodies sway to life's rhythm and rhyme,
Creating memories that last, a love sublime.

~ *Dorcas Chigodho*

HEARTBREAK

My heart is a canvas, torn apart
By the brushstrokes of love's dark art
The colors bleed, the edges fray
A masterpiece of pain, in shades of gray.

You're the ghost that haunts my mind
A whispered promise, left behind
A fragment of a love that's lost its way
A memory that refuses to fade.

In this silence, I'm a shipwrecked soul
Adrift on a sea of heartache's roll
The waves crash strong, the tides are cold
I'm searching for a shore to call my own.

My heart is a puzzle, broken and worn
The pieces scattered, the love that's torn
I'm trying to mend, to heal and to mend
But the scars remain, a love that won't end.

~Dorcas Chigodho

11. Blessy Rani Jenefer.S

Old Yet Golden | Artiverse

An IT Professional and Passionate writer who co-authored 70+ Anthologies, compiled her 12 own Anthologies and Head Compiled 7 Anthologies at various publications **in** different themes**. She** was honoured for her writings with many writer awards with different titles from 2021 to till now**.** She expresses her feelings & emotions through her writings. She continues to write while taking the time to indulge in her other hobbies like drawing**. B**eing a good dancer**,** one might even say she dances her way to a better life.

Her creative milestone was marked by the release of her first solo book "The Archive of Almost", a deeply person- al and evocative work that showcases her unique voice and storytelling prowess.

Instagram: @connect_with_quotes_
Email: sblessywriter@gmail.com

The Quiet After You

I don't cry like I used to do,
The tears now fall in shades of blue.
No thunder in my chest remains,
Just soft, relentless autumn rains.

Your name still echoes in my mind,
A song that time refused to bind.
I hum it low when no one's near,
A lullaby of loss and fear.

The coffee brews, but tastes like dust,
The mornings bloom, but not with trust.
I wear the smile you left behind,
It fits, but frays around the mind.

I scroll through photos, blurred and bent,
Each frame a ghost, each laugh a dent.
You look so real, so close, so gone,
A shadow stitched into the dawn.

And though I walk, and breathe, and try,
There's still a tremble in goodbye.
For love once held, then torn in two,
Leaves silence louder than it knew.

Yet in the hush, a seed remains,
A pulse beneath the grief and stains.
Though love has left its jagged mark,
I carry light inside the dark.

~Blessy Rani Jenefer.S

12. **Tatenda Alphapoet Bonga**

Old Yet Golden | Artiverse

Tatenda alphapoet Bonga is a freelancer writer and a song writer.

Email: newthornbornface@gmail.com

To Love A Broken Heart (Wasted)

Old Yet Golden | Artiverse

our souls undefined
bad habits
sometimes i start writing
that's death to words unsaid

in quiet jungles, a mourn of your pain
i heard, that filled terror of creature's absence
fractured ribs, pinned heart's broken pieces
with no sorry

found ourselves a birthmark
a coup from the world 'I'm Sorry'
we dipped pointy fingers
of boiling waters from our own arguments
so I've been trying to love you
back and forth

#farfromthevillage

13. **Subholaxmi Ganguly**

She passed class 12 ISC with 97.75 in humanities with a hundred in history. Passed class 10 ICSE with 95.2 percent with a century in chemistry. **S**he lives in Neam- atpur, Paschim Burdawan, West Bengal. Her father Sujan Ganguly, mother Sudipta Ganguly, younger sister Sudarshana Ganguly and many others (relatives, teach- ers and friends) are her sources of motivation. She writes both in English and in her mother tongue Bengali. 25+ of her Bengali poems have been publish- ed in a reputed newspaper called 'Ananda Bajar Potrika' and many of her English poems have been featured in 1 online app called Muzzer's homepage. She writes on varied subjects and also loves recitation. Her first poem drew it's inspiration from the struggling yet fighting world during the covid pandemics. **H**ope her poems inspire all. **W**ishing everyone all the very best for all their future endeavors. Signing off with a quote by DR. APJ Abdul Kalam who says "We are all born with a divine fire in us" Thanks and gratitude - Subholaxmi Ganguly

Email: subholaxmigangul@gmail.com
Insta: subholaxmi_here_1612

An Irreplaceable Bond

United we stand, with our heads held high,
Our family is strong with nothing to sigh.
Laughter and cries are a part of our life,
We slay all evils with our well - sharped knife.

From naughtiness to cracking jokes, we enjoy things happily,
After all, "Class 12" is a well - bonded family.
We have shoulders to rest our stressed heads on,
For we love each other immensely, in tons.

Punishments become sweet with this ever - gleeful group,
Marching towards our goals together like a cheerful troupe.
We may go apart in our very new futures,
But, we promise to be together until Earth ruptures.

~ *Subholaxmi Gangul*

14. **Amena Bhura**

Amena Bhura is a 17-year-old girl with a deep passion for writing and literature. She finds joy in expressing her thoughts through short stories and poems, often weaving together imagination and reality with a unique creative touch. Beyond literature, Amena is a keen observer of people and everyday life, drawing inspiration from even the smallest details around her. Her ability to blend real experiences with fictional elements allows her to create work that feels both relatable and thoughtful. Curious and reflective by nature, she uses writing not only as a medium of creativity but also as a way to explore emotions, relationships, and the world within and around her.
Bhuraamena@gmail.com

In the corners of a dusty drawer,
Photographs quietly breathe.
The colours may have faded,
But the moments still gleam.

The sparkling laughs with unforgettable memory,
Now fade into aching cries.
While those silly fights, bursting with unleashed energy,
Echo now as tender smiles.

Like pressed flowers in a faded book,
They lie silent, fragile, and true.
Colours dimmed, but fragrance lingers,
Whispering days I once knew.

Like a faithful pet,
Memories never lose the map of
tender corners of time where I linked.
No matter how far they are,
They return with unerring instinct.

Weaving with the golden thread,
The fabric of who I am today.
Though long since shed,
They glow brighter day by day.

How double-faced memories are!
Some drift like a soft blanket on a cold night,

Wrapping you in tender comfort.
While others rise as a silent fight,
Stealing away that gentle comfort.

The tree was once just a tiny sprout,
With time it grew, its roots spread out.
Now aged and strong, its branches wide,
So are the memories that abide with us.

~Amena Bhura

15. **Miriam Sam**

Old Yet Golden | Artiverse

Graduation - Electronics and Communication Engineering ,Post graduation - MBA in Operations and Marketing.

Email: miriamsam1997@gmail.com
Insta: merinmiriam_555

Friendship

A bond, so pure

Irreplaceable by anything else

Gives hope beyond words

Teaches you the joy of sharing and caring

~Miriam Sam

16. **Stoic Vin**

Stoic Vin is a poet and writer who finds inspiration in life's quiet truths, fleeting emotions, and the unspoken depth of human connections. His writings often explore themes of love, loss, healing, and self-discovery. For him, writing is not just a passion—it is a journey : a way to capture moments, embrace honesty, and connect with souls beyond boundaries.

Email: stoicvin14@gmail.com
Insta: stoic_vin

<u>*Bougainvillea*</u>

You gave me a flower that day,
Not for show, not just to say.
It was Bougainvillea, bright and wild,
Something soft, but strong and styled.

No wrapper, no ribbon, nothing grand,
Just a bloom resting in your hand.
But in that moment, I saw something more—
A quiet feeling I hadn't felt before.

No big drama, no fancy show,
Just petals speaking what words don't know.
A small gesture, but it felt so deep—
A memory now, that I'll quietly keep

It wasn't love in a filmi way,
Just a calm, like the end of the day.
As if you saw through my silent smile,
And chose to sit there, just for a while.

The petals weren't perfect—some were torn,
But they felt real, like mornings worn.
A small gesture, not meant to stay,
Yet somehow, it still finds its way.

You came gently, without a sound,
No promises made, no roots in the ground.
We spoke, we laughed, hearts open wide,
But time, as always, slipped outside.

That flower—maybe you gave it just like that,
A simple thing, no meaning exact.
But I held it close, without a clue,
That I wouldn't get another from you.

Then days passed by, like drifting sand,
And life moved on, as life had planned.
We never met again—not by fight or choice,
Just distance growing without a voice.

And sometimes I wonder—do you feel it too?
The Bougainvillea…. and that silent 'thank you.

Now whenever I see that flower in view,
I pause a moment—just thinking of you.

Later, life moved on.
A year later, I found it between pages—
Pressed petals,
colourless, brittle, almost breaking.
Just like what we had.
Still there.
Still hurting.
Still holding every emotion.

~ Stoic Vin

17. **Anukul Bansal**

Old Yet Golden | Artiverse

Anukul is a mechanical engineer who gave up his job to pick up pen to give magic to the silent words!

Email:hansum.dude143@gmail.com
Insta id : - novice_wordsmith1

Friendship

Old Yet Golden | Artiverse

Life is fickle and tickling down with memories
Friendship is a world which abates storms.
The rooster of Friendship is based on trust
Layer of each affirmations causes the unknown crust

Friendship is grown with maturity and age
the only mode without any stress cage

Inductive redesigned by the harsh realities
roof of darkness found happiness accessories

Waining energy doesn't fade
Inking stories about our relationship on a silver page

Together we enjoy the different shades and hues
hugs are a part of their bag full of vibrant vibes!

A festival glittered with happiness
dew which doesn't allow any stress and darkness

Escaping the tension chord
detachment within the gospel that should be discard

~Anukul Bansal

18. **Suchismita Sahoo**

Old Yet Golden | Artiverse

Suchismita Sahoo is a connoisseur of words, a seeker of stories, and a devotee of poetry. With an M.A. in English, she immerses herself in the boundless realm of literature, losing herself in its beauty, passion, and depth. Her soul blooms like a rare flower in the vast garden of letters, where every reader, like a delicate butterfly, can alight upon **her** verses and sip the nectar of her imagination. She does not merely write; she breathes **life** into words, crafting **a** sanctuary where stories and poetry dance in eternal harmony.

Email: suchismitasahoo640@gmail.com

Hey! The man of my Heart!

Thanks for stepping into my life,
Thanks for straining my life,
And converting it from darkness to light.
Should I bow down in front of you?

Nevertheless! It will be nothing to me

Hey! The king of my Soul!

Thanks for jewelling me with a beautiful love mole,
Thanks for criticizing me to prioritize my role.
Should I hug you tight , to make you delight?

Nevertheless! It will be nothing to me.

Hey! The Duke of my Empire!

A big thanks to you for arriving into my life,
Turning my tears into a pearl of file,
and collecting my happiness as golden pantiles.

Love you for your incredible Sacrifice.
Thanks to God for gifting you in my life.

-Suchismita ♡

19. **Aakaash Chaudhary**

Yet discovering myself

Golden Years

Golden years, like sunset's glow
Wisdom and love, forever grow
In wrinkled hands, a story's told
Of memories, young and old

The past shines bright, like gold refined
Lessons learned, and love defined
In every line, a tale is spun
Of trials faced, and victories won

Though time may fade, the years go by
The heart remains, with love that never dies
Old yet golden, like a treasure rare
A life well-lived, with love to share.

~Aakaash Chaudhary

Timeless Treasure

Golden hues of sunset fade
As twilight whispers, a gentle shade
The stars appear, like diamonds bright
A night of peace, in the golden light

The years go by, like falling leaves
But memories remain, in golden eaves
The heart remembers, the love so true
A treasure trove, of moments anew

In the golden glow, of a bygone age
Lies the wisdom, of a timeless stage
Where love and laughter, forever stay
A golden legacy that never fades away.

~Aakaash Chaudhary

20. Rakesh Mondal

Rakesh, 21, is a passionate writer and a science student whose words carry both simplicity and depth, touching the hearts of readers with raw emotion. He has been featured in over 30 anthologies and has won first prizes in many prestigious writing contests, establishing himself as a consistent and inspiring literary voice. He is also the author of the solo poetry collection Empty Canvas Talks, available on Lulu and Amazon, where he paints silence, hope, and life's hidden emotions onto the canvas of words. Beyond achievements, writing remains his journey of self-expression, and through every page he pens, he is still discovering life and its lessons, the beauty and the pain, the light and the silence within.

Email: rakesht0816@gmail.com
Insta: _rakeshzz_

When Memories Stay

The room still smells of you,

like the evening after rain,
soft, heavy, and unforgotten.
I sit where you used to sit,
and the air hums with echoes
of laughter that time stole.

Your shadow lingers in corners,
a quiet companion to my solitude.
I remember every smile,
every word that slipped between us,
and even the silence
that once felt like comfort
now aches like a wound...

Photographs stare back,
smiling faces frozen in light,
and I trace them with trembling hands,
knowing some moments
are meant to live forever,
even if the hearts that made them
can no longer hold each other..

I wander through these memories
like a traveler lost at dusk,
searching for a path that no longer exists.
Yet, in every pang of loss,
in every shadow of pain,
I find pieces of you
that will never leave-
because love, even broken,
refuses to vanish completely...

©Rakesh

<u>*Ashes of Us*</u>

The room still breathes your absence,
a quiet rhythm that matches my own broken pulse.

I see you in the corners of shadows,
in the spaces between raindrops,
in the hush of mornings that refuse to be gentle.

Your laughter, once a fire in my chest,
now flickers like dying embers,
scattering memories that cut deeper than any knife
could.
I trace your name on fogged windows,
on old photographs, on the air you used to touch,
and every trace burns like a confession I cannot speak.

I wander through the streets of our past,
barefoot on shattered dreams,
searching for the pieces of you that slipped through my
fingers like smoke,
and even when I find a fragment,
it disappears in my trembling hands.

Time has not healed me;
it has only taught me to carry this hollow weight,
to cradle the ache of a love that refuses to die,
to live in the ghost of us without ever seeing you again.

Even now, when the world moves on,
even when your eyes forget mine,

I feel you, a quiet storm in my chest,
an echo that refuses to vanish, a heartbreak that is still,
somehow, all I have learned to love…

©Rakesh

21. G. Sree Mathi

Ms. G.Sree Mathi is a poet and writer, and the daughter of Mr. G. Ganesan and Mrs. M. Hemalatha. Her journey with the English language has been both inspiring and fulfilling, shaped by a deep passion for learning and communication. She holds a Master of Arts in English, a Bachelor of Education, a Diploma in Communication and Functional English, and a Diploma in Gandhian Thought. At present, Ms. Sree Mathi serves as an Assistant Professor of English at N.M.S. Sermathai Vasan College for Women, Madurai. She began her professional journey as a language trainer at Canbridge English Academy, where she laid the foundation for her teaching career. She extends her heartfelt gratitude to her family, friends, publisher, and printer for their constant support and encouragement in her literary journey.

Email: manisree176@gmail.com

Scars That Still Shine

I gave my heart, so pure, so true,
Built dreams of forever, all painted in you.
Your words were promises, sweet as the rain,
Yet love left me standing in echoes of pain.

I trusted your smile, I believed your eyes,
But truth was hidden beneath gentle lies.
The laughter we shared now whispers in vain,
Each memory burns, yet teaches through pain.

I walked through darkness, drowning in tears,
Haunted by love, by hopes, by fears.
But broken hearts learn to glow once more,
For strength is born when we hit the floor.

I found myself where love once bled,
In every tear that my soul has shed.
Now I rise—not to forget, but to grow,
For even in loss, new seeds will sow.

Love failed, but I did not fall apart,
I rebuilt my dreams, rewrote my heart.
What once was sorrow now fuels my flame,
I walk with pride, no longer in shame.

For heartbreak is not the end, you see—
It's the start of becoming me.
~G. Sree Mathi

22. **Goldi Singh**

Old Yet Golden | Artiverse

Goldi Singh is a young passionate writer and compiler from the Gopalganj district of Bihar. Goldi began their writing journey in 2023. Their words carry a singular and profound mission, captured in their motto: "Ek ek alfaz, ab kare rooh se baat" (Every single word now speaks to the soul).

Email:goldisingh25112010@gmail.com
Insta :@the.goldisingh

I Wish Even Now

I wish even now
I wish even now
That old way of talking was still there
That old smile was still there
There were a thousand joys
I wish even now
That old trust was still there
That old hope was still there
There was no need for a scene (or a view/spectacle)
I wish even now
Everything that exists
Was all an ocean (boundless)
And the time that passed was itself a 'Wish'
I wish even now
The friends were the old ones
They were still the reason for the smile

~Goldi Singh

23. **Dr. Kokilavardhini Madhu**

Dr. Kokilavardhini Madhu, known by her pen name Bharathi, is a passionate writer with a background in M.Sc., B.Ed.,in Geography and DCA. **A** simple writer at heart, she pours her inner emotions into her words, turning them into heartfelt stories that resonate deeply with readers. Beyond writing, Bharathi is a multi- talented individual with achievements in singing, danc- ing, drawing and writing, having won several prizes at interschool and intercollege competitions. **S**he also served as an NSS volunteer, an experience that shaped her values of service, discipline, and resilience. Though family support was limited, Bharathi never gave up on her path. Through perseverance, she taught herself many lessons of life, carrying strength and hope into her creative journey. Her greatest longing has always been to publish a **book** of her own, while also aspiring for a fulfilling teaching career to inspire and guide young minds. For her, writing is more than art—it is the voice of her soul, a reflection of struggles, dreams, and emotions that define her.

Email: mayamadhumyk@gmail.com
Insta: Drbharathi_203711

Heartbreak

A thousand dreams now turned to dust,
The words we shared have lost their trust.
The smile once warm now fades away,
Like twilight stealing at the end of day.

I held your hand through storm and rain,
Yet here I stand, alone in pain.
Your voice still echoes soft and near,
But only silence answers here.

The stars we named have lost their glow,
Their light now mocks the ache I know.
The love once pure, now torn apart,
Leaves bleeding edges on my heart.

Time may move on, but scars remain,
A quiet song of tender pain.
For love once gone can't be replaced,
It lingers still — a ghost embraced.

~Dr. Kokilavardhini Madhu

24. **Bindu**

A home manager who likes to read, scribble poems, quotes on nature and life, sometimes tries jotting down short stories. Loves driving and taking short trips to places of nature.

Email: bindusarajacob@gmail.com
Insta : joys_and_nature

Memories of yesteryear
Chucking away to elsewhere
To the place I can't go back
That have been stuck deep in my heart.

That cashew tree
That curvy grass path to run free
That stand alone well
Those cows and goats with ringing bells
That warm tight hug from the wrinkled arms

Where have they all gone?

Memories of yesteryear
I want to go back that far
Just to have a glimpse
Of the things that I missed out in jiff
To take in my soul all I sought
To again hug back the cuddly warm heart.

-Bindu

25. Mrs.P.ShanmugaPreethi

Mrs.P.ShanmugaPreethi, is a daughter of Pandi Selvam & Parimala, Wife of Nagarajan, Enthusiastic, Dynamic, Poetess, Writer, Compiler, An Assistant Professor by trade with a Master of Philosophy in English, Master of Arts, Bachelor of Education, Diploma & Advanced Diploma in Communicative and Functional English, Diploma in Gandhian Thought, has been teaching English Language and Literature for ten years in N.M.S. Sermathai Vasan College For Women, Madurai, have completed NPTEL Course on "Effective Writing", have got Achiever Award for English Literature, author of the book "U n h e a r d R h y t h m s" under the title "Unsaid Feeling" published in conscience works publication, "Eternal Memories" published in The Little

Booktique Hub, a compiler of 'Identity' anthology published in Words Genix Publication, a compiler of 'Relationship', a compiler of 'Harmony of Heart Beat' &

'The Masters of Love' in Yahwah Publication (this anthology) and a co-author of 80 poems, in her point of view Tamil language is her emotion but English Language is her passion, have attended seminars, presented **8** papers**,** have published nearly **6** Research articles, proceedings with **ISBN & ISSN**, hobbies are Reading Magazines, blog postings, Articles.

Email : shanmugapreethi1992@gmail.com
Insta I'd: Eng shan pre

Love- Old yet Golden

Falling down is not only in land but also in love.,
Listening to old songs is how beautiful.,
Like my love feel beautiful .,
How simple my lover boy.,
How simple as our memories go on.,
I keep golden memories with you.,
But I will never forget our fights in silver memories.,
The portrait of ours is a golden one.
Whether it may be black and white or colour.,
You always have a golden heart.,
You join hands with silvery minds.,
We updated the versions from old to gold.
Old Jewellery collection is how much time spent.,
Old ones never fade anymore.,
We become old as our love is never old.,
We have a little break to recreate the memories.,
How we see our world old to golden one.

~ Mrs.P.ShanmugaPreethi

26. **Dr. Rutam Biswal**

Dr. Rutam Biswal is a passionate scholar, researcher, and writer. Her academic journey has been marked by consistent excellence—beginning with top ranks in CBSE board exams and culminating in prestigious national fellowships like the DST-INSPIRE (JRF & SRF), CSIR-NET (Rank 29) and GATE. Her research explores innovative materials and their applications, blending modern science with a keen interest in India's traditional knowledge systems. Beyond the laboratory, Dr. Biswal has carved a niche in creative and academic writing. She has won over 30 awards in national and institutional essay contests, including multiple first prizes in the Competition Success Review (CSR) essay series, and the First Prize in the National Research Paper Writing Competition—Vision for Viksit Bharat (2024). Her work reflects a deep commitment to bridging science, culture, and literature. With a drive for discovery and a love for language, she continues to contribute meaningfully to both scientific and literary communities.

Old Yet Golden

Beneath the dust of passing years,
Lie whispers soft, of joy and tears,
Of letters faded, edges torn,
Yet hearts still bloom where love was born.

We walked through sunsets, hand in hand,
No need for words to understand,
The silence spoke, the stars would gleam,
You were the echo of my dream.

Time played its tune, both harsh and kind,
But left your fragrance in my mind,
The laughter shared, the foolish fights,
Still glow within my soul's dim lights.

We parted ways, yet not apart,
You built a home inside my heart,
The seasons changed, the colors flew,
But some things stay — like love once true.

And though the mirrors mock my age,
My heart still writes you on its page,
For some sweet tales are never old,
They turn to gold — when time turns cold.

Echoes of the Unsaid

Remember those nights of endless talk,
Our dreams stretched far on that old park walk,
We laughed at stars, we feared no fall,
Two souls, one world — we had it all.

Your words were wings to my heavy heart,
Your smile a balm when life fell apart,
We built a world of hopes so wide,
Till silence crept and love had died.

Not every bond is meant to stay,
Some fade, like mist, with light of day,
Yet still, when rain taps windowpanes,
I hear your voice through old refrains.

If time could mend what hearts had known,
We'd never have to walk alone,
But pain too blooms, as memories do,
It hurts — because it once was true.

Old laughter lingers, soft and kind,
In hidden corners of the mind,
Though friendship's thread may break or bend,
Its glow remains — that has no end.

~Dr. Rutam Biswal

27. **Yash Devlalikar**

Hello, my name is Yash Devlalikar
Email: yyashdevlalikar@gmail.com
Insta: yash_devlalikar_quotes

The Journey of my Life

Trust me when I say-when it is right, everything that you love ruthlessly will love you back with the same convic- tion. Trust me when I say-when it is right, the things you reach for in life, the things you deeply hope for, they will reach back. And I promise you, when that happens you will understand that all of the things you ached for that did not work out, all of the hearts that failed to appre- ciate the home you made for them inside of yourself, they were not the things that broke you, or ruined you, or made you less worthy.

No, instead, you will see that they built you. They taught you about yourself. They led you to the person you were born to be, and they guided you to the person you were meant to be with. They shaped you. They challenged you. They grew you.

28. **ManjuAnand**

Ms Manju Anand was born into a modest family **in** Rohtak **to** the late Usha Anand and Jagdish Anand. She grew up in a joint family, being the only girl. From a young age, she displayed exceptional academic abilities and consistently topped her school. Tragically, her mother Usha Anand passed away on 16 August, 2017, leaving a profound impact on Ms ManjuAnand and her family. Faced with finacial difficulties, she took on the role of a teacher to support herself and contribute to her family's wel l being. Despite the challenges, Ms. Manju Anand nurtured numerous aspirations and had a deep sense of respon- sibility towards her family. She pursued her education, achieving the degrees of D.Ed, B.Sc (Non-Med), M.A (Eng) and B.Ed. Teaching children became her passion and she wholeheartedly dedicated herself to this noble profession. Alongside her commit- ment to education, MsManju Anand holds a strong faith

in God and embraces spirituality in her life. She received training **in** Rajyoga from Mount Abu, further enhancing her spiritual journey. In pursuit of professional develop**-** ment, she attended the National Seminar **of** Maths conducted **by** Dr. A.P Chawala. Ms.Manju Anand's dedication **and** innovative teaching methods have earned **her** recognition **and** accolades. **She** has been honoured with awards from **este**emed institutions such as Bharat Vikas Prashid, Batra Memorial Award and Teacher Innovation award by Sri Aurobindo Society.She has been bestowed **with** the National Innovative
Teacher Award from Haryana by Balrakshak Pratisthan, highlighting her exemplary contributions to education. Ms Manju Anand's journey is a testament to her persev- erance, love for teaching and belief in spirituality. Her accomplishments and commitment to her profession continue to inspire both her students and peers alike.

Email: manjuanand94@gmail.com
Insta: manjuanand_507

Old is Gold

Day by day are passing away
Black hair has turned into white
Our parents are getting old,
But their hands has magic to make life bright.

Went to the houses of relatives,
By walking and sitting on bicycle.
Time has passed away,
Went for an hour,
By riding the car.

Fresh fruits and vegetables gave health,
Snacks and cold drinks are giving to all' death'.

No doubt, old is gold.
Past lifestyle is better than today.
Respect for parents and teachers,
With the passage of time going away.

Till there is time,
Respect your elders.
Keep the moral values of your elders.
Life will be like a gold necklace.

~ManjuAnand

29. **Rengasri R**

Rengasri R is an avid writer and learner who enjoys compiling and coauthoring anthologies.

Email: Bajrangbaan720@gmail.com

Threads of Reality

Some dresses, worn with time's embrace,
Still shimmer with a golden trace,
Whispers of laughter, tears once shed,
Threads of stories long since read.

Not just fabric, but fragments of me,
Each crease a memory, wild and free,
A tear, a mark, a stain so dear,
Holding moments I hold near.

Raised to cherish what we own,
In broken mugs, in hearts unknown,
The things we discard today,
Once filled with joy, now fade away.

But in the rush to let them go,
We forget the love they used to show,
The hands that held, the dreams they wore,
The life they lived—who could ask for more?

Now, in stillness, I see the truth,
These things are more than age or youth.
They transform, they don't decay,
They hold our past in every way.

In a world that moves too fast,
The truest wisdom lies in the past—
Some things are meant not to replace,
But to remember, and to embrace.

Rengasri R

30. **B. Raj Kumar**

B.Raj Kumar an electrical engineer by qualification has 35 years of work experience spanning various industries. **He** wants **to** pursue his passion of writing poetry and novels in English as his 2nd career.

Insta ID: balasubramaniyan.rajkumar.

Old Memories

I bit into my single toffee,
I shared it with my classmate like coffee.

I ran out of ink during the exam,
He lent me a drop, asking what harm?

Will those good old days ever come back?
Has not life made us lose track?

The happiness that first love gave,
Her small, small items that I did save.

The notes that I wrote down for her,
That she accepted with a smile, going no further.

Today as we meet after 25 years,
Still unable to hug her and let go my fears.

~B.Raj Kumar.

www.ingramcontent.com/pod-product-compliance
Ingram Content Group UK Ltd.
Pitfield, Milton Keynes, MK11 3LW, UK
UKHW021409190726
13845UKWH00028B/987

9 788199 664234